A LIFE FORCE

BY Will Eisner

DC COMICS

New York, New York

A LIFE FORCE

WILL EISNER
writer and artist

Published by DC Comics, 1700 Broadway, New York, NY 10019.
A division of Warner Bros. - An AOL Time Warner Company.
Visit our website at www.dccomics.com

Printed and bound in Canada.

ISBN: 1-56389-789-X

First DC Comics printing August 2001

AFTER THE CRASH OF THE STOCK MARKET IN 1929
A GREAT DEPRESSION
ENGULFED WESTERN SOCIETY LIKE A GREY CLOUD!
SUDDENLY IT SEEMED,
TO A WORLD WHICH HAD BEEN IN GLEEFUL PURSUIT
OF THE GOOD LIFE,
THAT LIVING HAD BECOME SURVIVAL!
MANY HITHERTO UNQUESTIONED ASSUMPTIONS NOW
CAME UNDER REEXAMINATION.
WHERE THEY COULD, PEOPLE RELOCATED
FROM FARM TO CITY OR CITY TO FARM....
SEEKING GREENER PASTURES LIKE HUNTER-GATHERERS OF OLD.
BUT IN THE BRONX, ON DROPSIE AVENUE,
MOST TENEMENT DWELLERS REMAINED
HOLDING FAST TO THEIR BEACH-HEAD
SIMPLY BECAUSE THEY HAD ONLY JUST ARRIVED
FROM OTHER MORE HOSTILE PLACES.
THEY CARRIED WITH THEM
THE TABERNACLE OF A LIFE FORCE
THEY HARDLY UNDERSTOOD.

...IT WAS NOW
THE MIDDLE THIRTIES...

EMPLOYMENT
AGENCY

3.

1934

" . . . the withered leaves of industrial enterprise lie on every side . . . the savings of many thousands of families are gone . . . unemployed citizens face the grim problem of existence. . . ."

FRANKLIN D. ROOSEVELT
From his first Inaugural Address

ITEMS FROM THE NEW YORK PRESS

1500 HOMELESS LIVE IN ARMORY

69th REGIMENT HOUSES POOR

FEB. 7, 1934

Sheltered from the cold, over 1500 homeless people have found at least temporary refuge in the 69th Regiment Armory at Lexington Avenue and Twenty-Sixth Street in New York.

These victims of the depression, poorly clothed and dispirted, have been pouring into the huge building filling the drill floor and the mezzanine. Coming from the inclement pavements and wet doorways or dank subway kiosks, they encamp on the polished wooden floors.

SIMPLE GAMES OCCUPY THEIR TIME

In an effort to keep up morale,the men play checkers, jigsaw puzzles and hang around a piano played by a volunteer of surprising talent.

SLUMP CAN AFFECT PEOPLE'S HEALTH

INCREASE IN ILLNESS AND REDUCTION OF INCOME EFFECT.

In an article published on Jan. 14 by the *New York Times,* it was reported that the average annual income of a representative group of American wage-earners dropped from $1700 in 1929 to $900 this year.

The significance of the statistic is that historically an economic depression usually results in sickness and impaired vitality.

RATE OF DEATH SINCE 1929 HAS REDUCED

Strangely enough, the U.S. death rate has fallen despite the drop in living standards.

TWO MEN FAINT OF HUNGER IN CITY HALL WHILE WOMAN SCREAMS

MAYOR LA GUARDIA HALTS CONFERENCE

MARCH 2, 1934

According to the *New York Times,* two men in a group of twenty-two unemployed people besieged City Hall in the belief that the mayor would give them jobs in snow removal work, collapsed in the hall outside the Mayor's Office.

Both men, exhausted from lack of food, were immediately taken to the Beekman Street Hospital at Mayor Fiorello La Guardia's orders.

"WANT JOBS, NOT FOOD"

The men had worked the day before at snow clearing for the Sanitation Department until they were laid off for lack of work.

CHAPTER 1.

IZZY
THE COCKROACH
AND
THE MEANING OF LIFE

THE TENEMENT AT 55 DROPSIE AVENUE
LAY QUIETLY AT ANCHOR IN ITS SEA OF CONCRETE.
THE SOUNDS OF THE CITY WERE DIMINISHING.
ALREADY ONE COULD HEAR RUSS COLUMBO SINGING
FROM A RADIO IN THE SECOND FLOOR BACK.
IT WAS FRIDAY AND IT WAS SUNDOWN,
AND THE LAST OF THE REGULAR CONGREGANTS
OF THE SYNAGOGUE ON THE NEXT BLOCK
WERE WALKING HOME.

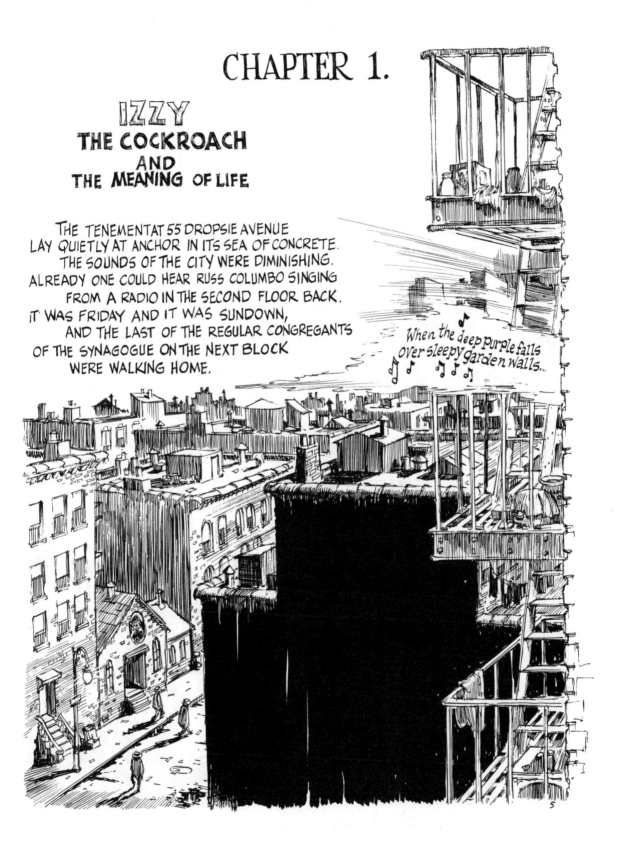

♪ ♪ When the deep purple falls
over sleepy garden walls...
♪ ♪ ♪ ♪

5

TWO...
RIFKA SHTARKAH PREPARED FOR THE SABBATH...

SO, WHERE IS JACOB? IT IS GETTING LATE, ALREADY!

IF... MAN CREATED GOD...

...THEN, THE REASON FOR LIFE IS ONLY IN THE MIND OF MAN! !!

...IF, ON THE OTHER HAND, GOD CREATED MAN...

THEN, THE REASON FOR LIVING IS STILL ONLY A GUESS!

...AFTER ALL IS SAID AND DONE...

WHO REALLY KNOWS THE WILL OF GOD??

......SO, IN EITHER CASE, BOTH MAN AND COCKROACH ARE IN SERIOUS TROUBLE! BECAUSE STAYING ALIVE SEEMS TO BE THE ONLY THING ON WHICH EVERYBODY AGREES!

18.

19

21

CHAPTER 2

ESCAPEE

SOUTH, SOUTHWEST- ACROSS THE HARLEM RIVER
WHERE THE BRONX ENDS, IS MANHATTAN ISLAND.
THERE...IS THE LAND OF PROMISE

DANIEL, SON OF JACOB,
MADE IT FROM DROPSIE AVENUE.
VIA NIGHT SCHOOL,
MEDICAL SCHOOL BY DAY
(DRIVING A TAXI BY NIGHT)
AND FINALLY
AN INTERN
AT MT. HEBRON HOSPITAL
MANHATTAN EAST SIDE.
DANIEL HAD **ESCAPED**...
INTO THE MAINSTREAM.

HELLO, MOMMA ... THIS IS DANIEL

25

CHAPTER 3.
ON THE TOP FLOOR, BACK, LIVED GOD

ON WEDNESDAY AFTERNOONS HEBREW LESSONS AND PREPARATION FOR BAR MITZVAH WERE CONDUCTED BY RABBI BENSOHN AT REDUCED PRICES FOR THOSE WHO COULD NOT AFFORD THE CHEDER.

SO... TODAY, FOR A CHANGE, YOU ARE ON TIME!

OOW, JEEZ, GOOMIE..!! WOT'LL I DO? ...I DINT STUDY MY LESSON... I'M-GONNA BE MOIRDERED !!

SO, PRAY FER A MIRACLE, VELVEL !! C'MON...

TO SIT AT THE FEET OF GOD IS AWESOME

HERE, MIRACLES COULD OCCUR...

SOMETIMES

33

35

HOW EVER MANKIND DEALT WITH ITS SURVIVAL, THERE REMAINED YET ANOTHER FORCE, MIGHTY AND IMPLACABLE... THE WEATHER!

JANUARY, 1934, ARRIVED TO A SLUSHY NEW YORK. It began mildly. A warm wave thawed the accumulation of snow that was deposited on the city in the month before. Firemen had to be called out to deal with floods caused by suddenly-thawed sprinklers in over 200 buildings. Meanwhile, 40,000 were given work to clear the snow. In the New York Harbor, fog, resulting from the sudden warmth, delayed ship traffic.

JANUARY ENDED IN SUDDEN COLD! The mercury dropped 52 degrees in one day and the thermometers of the city stood at 5 degrees above zero with icy winds and snow flurries swirling around the buildings.

FEBRUARY BEGAN AFTER THREE DAYS OF BITTER COLD. Warm winds brought relief, just briefly, for a heavy snowfall buried the city! While 2000 worked at shovelling streets and 20,000 out-of-work people eagerly awaited a chance for a job, bad news came from the Bronx! At the Bronx Zoo the groundhogs failed to come out! Those who counted on these creatures to predict spring were bitterly disappointed. Then the temperature dropped to 15 degrees and a pile-up of 9.6 inches of snow giving employment to the 20,000 jobless at snow removal.

ON FEBRUARY 2, THERE WAS OTHER GOOD NEWS! Up in the Bronx Zoo the groundhog finally came out, saw his shadow, and promptly scurried back to his nest. It was clearly a portend of an early spring. But by the day's end the mercury dropped to 4 degrees . . . a record for this date.

ON FEBRUARY 3RD ICE FLOES RAMPANT ON THE HUDSON RIVER! Propelled by the currents they dragged three ships for twenty blocks from their anchorage.

ON FEBRUARY 13 THE CITY WAS LASHED BY A BITTER GALE FOLLOWED BY A HEAVY SNOWFALL! Within eleven hours the mercury dropped 20 degrees. On the rivers the Coast Guard struggled to save men on barges adrift on the icy waters. But the snowfall gave work to 6000 jobless men hired to clean streets.

ON FEBRUARY 15, N.Y. BRACED FOR ANOTHER COLD. The New York Times reported that a cold wave was coming from the Rocky Mountains and that an unemployed man was found dead of the cold alongside a bunkmate who was unconscious. The following day the paper reported that the first half of February was the coldest in the 63 years of the New York City Weather Bureau's records.

ON FEBRUARY 20, THE CITY WAS HIT AGAIN! After almost a week of wavering the mercury dropped to 9 degrees above zero and a 9-inch snowfall immobilized the city. For hours the suburbs were cut off. Suburbanites in snow shoes and skies were also using horses and sleds to get around.

ON FEBRUARY 22, N.Y. WAS PINIONED BY SNOW! The city's newspapers carried stories of milk being delivered to the suburbs by plane. In the city itself 50,000 people were at work digging out. Slowly, commuters were able to get back to work. In the New York Times an expert, Mr. Raubenheimer, called the storm ". . . a carbon copy of the Blizzard of 1888."

BY FEBRUARY 27, THE CITY TRIED TO FREE ITSELF! After a day or two of rising and falling temperature which caused icy streets that was soon covered by a 9-inch snowfall, the papers carried reports that some Long Island and New Jersey communities were cut off from the city. In Manhattan hotels were jammed with snowbound commuters. Only the busses were running. Nine storm-related injuries were reported. The following day the total fatalities related to the thermometer rose to 14. Stores announced that skis and earmuffs sold out! The mercury dropped to 9 degrees above zero but the city somehow averted a coal and food shortage, fed its park animals, while in Westchester County the roads were cleared.

MARCH CAME IN LIKE A LAMB THIS YEAR. With a 15 degree rise in temperature which caused a thaw that melted the accumulated ice, water flooded the streets of the city.

ON APRIL 24, THE CITY FELT THE FIRST THUNDERSTORM OF THE YEAR!

BY MAY 21, THE CITY SWELTERED! A record heat of 88 degrees Farenheit roasted the city and left one heat prostration case. This was followed by hail, rain and lightning which caused damage and resulted in 3 prostrations within 72 hours.

JULY ARRIVED WITH THE MERCURY AT 91 DEGREES. Within the next three days 13 more heat prostrations and 5 deaths were reported in the press before a rainstorm finally brought a short relief. But the mercury hovered at over 92 degrees for the next eight days leaving about 12 overcome and 3 dead.

ST. SWITHEN'S DAY WAS SULTRY and ended in showers.

JULY ENDED WITH THE MERCURY AT 89 DEGREES. A count of the heat-related casualties which the New York Times reported for the month came to 29 prostrations and 11 deaths. Two heat records were set they said.

AUGUST BEGAN, RECORDING THE COOLEST AUGUST 6 IN HISTORY. At the end of the month, after zooming up to 95 degrees, the month ended with the coolest day in August's history.

FINALLY, BY DECEMBER   New York returned to a seasonal norm and a light snow powdered the rooftops.

• • • •

NEVERTHELESS, THE COCKROACHES IN THE TENEMENTS ON DROPSIE AVENUE RESPONDING TO A LIFE FORCE EQUAL TO THE ENVIRONMENT, CONTINUED THEIR PROLIFERATION AS THEY HAD FOR OVER FOUR MILLION YEARS!

CHAPTER 4
SHABBASGOY

THE SHAFTSBURYS EMIGRATED TO NEW ENGLAND IN 1850. THERE THEY FOUNDED AN AXE-HANDLE FACTORY WHICH FLOURISHED. IT REMAINED IN THE FAMILY'S HANDS UNTIL THE DEATH OF ELTON JOSIAH SHAFTSBURY AROUND 1927.

HIS SON, ELTON SHAFTSBURY II HIS ONLY HEIR, THEN TOOK OVER THE OPERATION OF THE SHAFTSBURY WOOD PRODUCTS COMPANY.

ACTUALLY, YOUNG ELTON HAD LITTLE INTEREST IN RUNNING A BUSINESS. HE HAD BEEN REARED IN COMFORT AND SECURITY. WITH AN UNQUESTIONED CONFIDENCE IN HIS SURVIVAL THAT CAME FROM THE CERTAINTY OF HIS SOCIAL POSITION, HE EXPECTED HIS WORLD TO GO ON, AS IT WAS, FOREVER. HIS SKILLS WERE MAINLY CENTERED IN THE ART OF BEING ACCEPTED AND THE MAINTENANCE OF THE SHALLOW RELATIONSHIPS THAT WERE NORMAL FOR HIS "SET".

WHAT ELTON SHAFTSBURY II REALLY WANTED WAS FREEDOM TO PURSUE HIS SOCIAL LIFE.

SO, UPON THE DEATH OF HIS FATHER, ELTON SOLD THE FACTORY AND PUT THE PROCEEDS INTO THE STOCK MARKET.

THIS ENABLED HIM TO ENGAGE IN A MORE 'GENTLEMANLY' VOCATION. HE JOINED A MAIN-LINE WALL STREET BROKERAGE HOUSE AND OCCUPIED HIMSELF WITH BEING A 'CUSTOMER'S-MAN'. HERE HIS SOCIAL CONTACTS AND RICH FRIENDS WERE AN ASSET THAT ALLOWED HIM TO MAKE MONEY IN A 'NICE WAY'!

IN THE FALL OF 1929, THE STOCK MARKET COLLAPSED, AND WITHIN MONTHS HIS HOLDINGS WERE WIPED OUT. THE BROKERAGE HOUSE, LIKE SO MANY OTHERS, COLLAPSED AND HIS CIRCLE OF FRIENDS SUFFERED SIMILARLY... THEY SOON DISPERSED.

ELTON'S LAST SAVINGS WERE DEMOLISHED IN THE FAILURE OF THE NOTORIOUS BANK OF U.S.

BY THE WINTER OF 1933 ELTON SHAFTSBURY II, BROKE AND UNEMPLOYED, WAS REDUCED TO SELLING APPLES ON THE CORNER OF WALL AND WILLIAM STREET.

1929

BYRD IN SAFE FLIGHT OVER SOUTH POLE

The N.Y. Times on Nov. 30 reported that Admiral Byrd, the first to conquer the North Pole, succeeded in flying over the South Pole as well.

President Herbert Hoover sent the aviator and his crew a congratulatory message that said in part ". . . we are glad of proof that the spirit of great adventure still lives."

Mayor Jimmy Walker, of New York said, ". . . the American flag will look great down there."

SOCIAL NOTE

BERLIN, OCT. 29

Fritz Von Opel, the first man to fly a rocket plane, revealed today, he would wed Frau Selnik who is one of Germany's six women pilots. They will come to New York in November.

STOCK MARKET DROPS 15 BILLION OCT. 29 SELL OFF WORST IN HISTORY 16,410,030 SHARES TRADED

EMBEZZLER GIVES UP $47,000 NAVY LOOT

BURIED IN D.C. CHICKEN YARD

OCT. 30, 1929

Lt. Charles Musil, U.S. Navy Paymaster surrendered to the authorities and led them to the cache in a chicken yard. However, $6,100 is still missing and the embezzler admits that he bought some stock before he became penitent and gave up.

BANKS OPTIMISTIC BUT SUPPORT FAILS

On Wednesday, Oct. 30, the New York press reported a major sell off of panic proportions on the previous day. By the end of trading, however, leading issues recovered as much as 14 points in 15 minutes to momentarily, at least, assuage the pall of gloom that overhung the financial centers.

RALLY BRIEF

Organized support from the leading financial houses is gathering to help offset the "mob psychology" that is blamed for the plunge.

1930

MURDER OF GAMBLER STILL UNSOLVED

FEB. 4, 1930

The New York Times in a special report revealed that the killing of Arnold Rothstein on Oct. 4, 1928 has precipitated an inquiry into the affairs of the city's magistrates courts, police department, and possibly fire department. Governor Franklin D. Roosevelt, when asked whether he would or would not veto an investigation, laughed, and said he would wait until he saw the legislation before deciding.

LINDBERGH SETS RECORD CROSSES U.S. IN 14½ HRS.

APRIL 20, 1930

Col. Charles A. Lindbergh added another first to his laurels by flying coast to coast, 14,000 feet at 180 mph. His wife served as navigator.

UNEMPLOYMENT ATTACKED IN SENATE

DEMOCRATS BLAME HOOVER'S POLICIES

MARCH 3, 1930

A major New York paper in an exclusive article reported that the Senate's Democratic leaders accused the Hoover Administration of diverting attention from the increase in unemployment. He questioned administration statistics.

"RECOVERY NEAR" DEPRESSION PEAK OVER SAYS HOOVER

"STOCK MARKET CRASH DUE TO SPECULATION ORGY BY PUBLIC"

MAY 1930

President Herbert Hoover in a statement to the press, said today that the programs he instituted succeeded in maintaining courage and confidence. The worst is over he feels.

CONDITIONS GROWING DAILY WORSE SAYS SENATOR LA FOLLETTE.

The Republican Senator from Wisconsin denounced attempts to label demonstrations by the unemployed as a movement by "The Reds." Another Republican guessed that unemployment stood at 6 million despite the questionably lower statistics from federal agencies.

300 N.Y. UNION LOCALS MEET IN MOVE TO COMBAT ACUTE UNEMPLOYMENT

MARCH 8, 1930

A meeting of major union locals in New York's Beethoven Hall will be held on March 19th.

38

1931

HUNGER RIOTS FAIL AS BRONX MARCH IS BROKEN UP BY COPS

JANUARY 9, 1931

In a demonstration that was reportedly staged by Communists in Manhattan, Brooklyn and the Bronx, police succeeded in easily dispersing what was termed as a "sparse" turnout.

At the Salvation Army's bread line on the Bowery at 4th Street, Manhattan, a policeman's jaw was broken.

STOCK MARKET UP

FEB. 17, 1931

The Stock Market rose 2-8 points yesterday on accumulating evidence of a business pickup. This followed a flurry of buying activity the week earlier when on Feb. 11, a rally from public buying sent the list up.

HOOVER WILL VETO BONUS BILL DESPITE SENATE PASSAGE

FEB. 20, 1931

The President, despite a vote in the Senate of 72-2 in favor of a loan bill for veterans' payments, warned that it would cause a weakening of the government's financial structure.

400,000 DEPOSITORS OF NY BANK OF U.S. FATE NOW IN DOUBT

REAL VALUE OF BANK'S ASSETS UNACCOUNTED

FEB. 2, 1931

The NY State Banking Dept. report issued yesterday was without a satisfactory account of the actual condition of the failed bank's assets. After weeks of liquidation, the books of the bank remain as cloudy as they were on the day it closed.

$75,000,000 of the closed bank's assets are apparently lost or at least cannot be accounted for.

HOUSE PAINTERS MAY USE NARROWER BRUSH TO CREATE MORE JOBS

FEB. 20, 1931

The New York Times carried a story today of a threat by the Painters Union of Long Island to go from the normal 6-inch paint brush to a smaller 3-inch brush so as to double the employment of housepainters in the city.

1932

F.D. ROOSEVELT WINS IN A LANDSLIDE ANTI-PROHIBITION CONGRESS NOW IN O'BRIEN BECOMES NEW YORK'S MAYOR

N.Y. CITY ASKS BANKS AID MAY DEFAULT CITY WAGE CUT $20,000,000

DEC. 7, 1932

The city faced an inevitable default on its obligations. Unless local bankers called on to rescue New York, said that the cut in city payrolls was not enough and urged that another $25,000,000 be cut in city spending before credit could be restored to permit their loan.

Meanwhile, members of the Patrolmen's Benevolent Assn. launched a drive to enlist public support against their pay cut.

SWARMS OF MOTHS BLANKET THE BRONX

JULY 9, 1932

By midnight last night, a blizzard of fluttering moths engulfed the Bronx and then headed on to include Manhattan, Queens and Brooklyn. According to the New York Times, these were a gypsy moth specie and in such great numbers that they halted auto traffic on Jerome Avenue and Pelham Parkway. The police, deluged with phone calls, said that they were at a loss as to just what they were expected to do about it.

DEMOCRATS CONTROL CONGRESS IN RECORD NATIONAL VOTE

ONLY SIX STATES VOTED FOR HERBERT HOOVER

NOV. 9, 1932

In his lead article in the New York Times, Arthur Krock said ". . . a political cataclysm unprecedented in the nation's history and produced by three years of Depression" elected Franklin Delano Roosevelt, President of the United States.

47

48

CHAPTER 5
THE BLACK HAND

BETWEEN 1861 AND 1934 THE POPULATION OF ITALY HAD A NATURAL INCREASE OF ABOUT 400,000 A YEAR. THE DENSITY OF ITS POPULATION AVERAGED ABOUT 359 PERSONS PER SQUARE MILE.

DURING THE YEARS AFTER WORLD WAR I, THE ECONOMY, ESPECIALLY IN SOUTHERN ITALY AND SICILY COULD BARELY SUPPORT ITS POPULATION. EMPLOYMENT WAS SO SCARCE THAT ONLY 150 DAYS OF WORK PER YEAR WAS THE AVERAGE. IN THE SOUTHERN FARM LANDS, MALARIA AND OTHER POVERTY-RELATED DISEASES KEPT PRODUCTIVITY LOW.

THE STRONG CENTRAL GOVERNMENT SET UP IN 1870 HAD LONG BEEN BESET BY LOCAL GROUPS THAT GREW OUT OF STRONG 'FAMILIES' WHO CONTROLLED REGIONS. SMUGGLING, PETTY CRIME AND CORRUPTION WAS RIFE. LOYALTY TO A 'FAMILY' OR A SECRET SOCIETY WAS A WAY OF LIFE.

SO, BETWEEN 1919 AND 1924 EMIGRATION SOARED...WITH AMERICA AS THE FAVORED DESTINATION.

IN 1920, ALONE, OVER 300,000 ITALIAN IMMIGRANTS ENTERED THE UNITED STATES.

FINALLY, IN 1924, THE U.S. IMMIGRATION ACT CUT THE TORRENT AND ESTABLISHED A QUOTA OF ONLY 3,845 ITALIAN IMMIGRANTS PER YEAR.

THEREAFTER, ABETTED BY THE POLICIES OF THE FASCIST GOVERNMENT, IMMIGRATION TO THE U.S. DWINDLED TO A TRICKLE. NOW, GETTING TO AMERICA BECAME A MATTER OF SOME SKILL AND 'CONNECTION'.

HERE, THE OLD WORLD 'FAMILY' GROUPS AND SECRET SOCIETIES CAME INTO IMPORTANCE. FOR A FEE, THEY WANGLED VISAS, BRIBED OFFICIALS... OR ACTUALLY SMUGGLED MANY IMMIGRANTS INTO THE COUNTRY.

ONCE HERE, THEY WERE OFTEN INDENTURED TO THE SMUGGLING 'FAMILIES'...OR AT LEAST IN HEAVY DEBT FOR THEIR PASSAGE FEE. THESE FEES WERE INVARIABLY COLLECTED.

ONE OF THE GROUPS, WITH SICILIAN ROOTS WAS **'THE BLACK HAND'.** THEY, LIKE THE MAFIA, WERE OLD HANDS AT DISCIPLINE AND ENFORCEMENT.

A BLACK HAND IMPRINT ON ONE'S DOOR OR ON A LETTER WAS A NOTICE THAT WAS NOT TAKEN LIGHTLY.

...TELL YOU WHAT, ANGELO... I GIVE YOU A JOB ...A GUY NAME OF SHAFTSBURY LIVES IN THIS HOUSE, HE'S A RUNNER FOR SMITH & WHITE! ...YOU KNOW HIM??

HE LIVES ONNA 3RD FLOOR, BACK.

GET **FRIENDLY** WITH HIM ...GET HIM TO TELL YOU WHENEVER HE DELIVERS NEGOTIABLE BONDS

WOT YOU GONNA DO?

IT'S NOT YOU BUSINESS, ANGELO!

YOU GONNA DO LIKE HE SAYS ...RIGHT, PISAN? BE NICE !!

SLAM

WHAT THEY WANT WITH YOU, ANGELO??

THEY WANT ME TO **TELL'EM** WHENEVER MR. SHAFTSBURY COMES HOME WITH HIS BAG!

WHY?

HE'S A RUNNER FOR A BROKER. ...HE CARRIES **BONDS** WORTH A LOTTA MONEY!

WHY THEY ASKIN' **YOU** TO DO THAT!?

I **OWE** PETE! HE PAID FOR MY PASSAGE OVER FROM ITALY...SO, I OWE HIM...**AND NOW** I GOTTA DO IT, SEE?

53

The ENCHANTED PRINCE

ONCE UPON A TIME, A YOUNG PRINCE WAS BORN IN THE BRONX... HIS NAME WAS AARON.
UNHAPPILY, SOMEWHERE IN THE DIVINE CAULDRON WHERE MYSTERIOUS FORCES FABRICATE LIFE, SOMETHING WENT AWRY FOR AARON, AND IN THE SOFT CIRCUITRY OF HIS BRAIN AN INFINITESIMAL WELDING FAILED!!
OH...IT WAS ONLY A TINY MICROGAP BETWEEN UNCONNECTED TISSUE... A LITTLE CELL, PERHAPS, THAT FAILED TO FORM, OR DIED TOO SOON!
BUT IT LEFT, FOREVER, A FLAWED ENGINE, AN IMPERFECT INSTRUMENT, INVISIBLE AND UNSUSPECTED, INSIDE A HEALTHY BODY.
SO AARON GREW UP HANDSOME AND BRIGHT A PRINCELING WHO SEEMED DESTINED TO INHERIT A SECURE PLACE IN THE KINGDOM OF HUMAN KIND.
THEN ONE DAY, IN EARLY MANHOOD, THE CHEMISTRY THAT FUELED HIS BRAIN COULD NO LONGER DEAL WITH THE FLAW AND A SHORT CIRCUIT OCCURRED, UNFELT, UNNOTICED BUT IRREVOCABLE!
GRADUALLY, UNREASONED, TERRIBLE FEAR MINGLED WITH GRANDIOSE DREAMS IN THE TURGID, BOILING PLASMA OF HIS MIND.
HIS INTELLECT FOUGHT FOR CONTROL AND THIS STRUGGLE BROUGHT HIM PAIN. SOON THE AGONY BECAME SO DEBILITATING THAT HE SUCCUMBED TO IT...AND HE WITHDREW INTO HIMSELF MORE AND MORE! AT LAST HE LOST TOUCH WITH REALITY.
IN TIME...THE PAIN SUBSIDED, LEAVING HIM WITH A NUMB FEAR OF PEOPLE.
FINALLY HE MOVED INTO 55 DROPSIE AVENUE WHERE HE COULD LIVE OUT HIS LIFE IN AN ANONYMITY COMMONLY PROVIDED BY THE TENEMENT WALLS AND SUSTAINED BY A SMALL REMITTANCE FROM A REMOTE RELATIVE.
IN THIS SANCTUARY HE COULD MAKE HIS OWN WORLD AND POPULATE IT WITH CREATURES OF HIS OWN INVENTION.
AARON WAS NOW, TRULY, A PRINCE IN AN ENCHANTED KINGDOM!

THE NEXT MORNING AARON AWOKE TO A SENSATION OF TRANQUILITY... SURPRISINGLY, THE THREATENING IMAGES HAD LEFT WITH THE NIGHT.

FOR THE FIRST TIME IN A LONG WHILE HE COULD LOOK UPON THE REAL WORLD WITHOUT FEAR...

THE REMISSION FROM THE CONSUMING AGONY LEFT HIM WITH A SENSE OF STRENGTH AND A FEELING OF CURIOSITY...

NOW HE COULD GO OUT INTO THE REAL WORLD TO FIND REALITY

...SO MUCH FOR REALITY!!

64

CHAPTER 7
THE REVOLUTIONARY

IN 1934 THE WINDS OF CHANGE
SWIRLED AROUND
55 DROPSIE AVENUE, THE BRONX.

SOCIALIST PARTY MASS MEETING BROKEN UP BY COMMUNISTS

MADISON SQUARE GARDEN RALLY IS SCENE OF WILD MELEE

FEB. 17, 1934

New York: A free-for-all, in which about 5000 communists tried to "capture" a mass meeting in Madison Square Garden, resulted in many injuries and broken chairs.

The meeting, scheduled by Socialists to protest the slaughter of Austrian Workers by Fascists, was attended by 20,000 persons and proceeded as scheduled until the communists made their way into the building and began throwing chairs, engaging in fist fights while otherwise interrupting the speakers. Clarance Hathaway, the communist leader, was finally subdued and thrown out into the street where, bleeding from the nose and face, he continued to address a crowd on the sidewalk on Forty-ninth Street.

COMMUNIST LITERATURE BANNED IN N.Y. PRISON

FEB. 1, 1934

The N.Y. Times reported that Warden Lewis E. Lawes of Sing Sing Prison ordered "certain current periodicals with communist tendencies" banned from the prison.

Periodicals such as The New Masses and the Labor Defender will be forbidden. "There are some things you cannot permit where there are feeble-minded and easily influenced persons around," he said.

Actually, there are five known, admitted communists in the Ossining Prison.

INTERNATIONAL COMMUNIST REVOLUTION IS FORECAST

MOSCOW MEETING PREDICTS WORLD-WIDE REVOLT AT HAND

FEB. 3, 1934

The Associated Press, in a dispatch filed today from Moscow, reported that a claim of victory for world communism was proclaimed by a Soviet party leader.

In his address to the All-Union Communist Party Congress, D.Z. Manuilsky declared, "The elements of a revolutionary crisis are growing everywhere. The forces of a proletarian revolution are increasing. Mass strikes, peasant's revolts and military rebellions ... herald the coming revolutions. Communists in all countries have learned to fight and conquer ... we will conquer the whole world."

REVOLUTIONARY JAILED FOR PAINTING "VOTE COMMUNIST" ON BRONX STREET

OCT. 28, 1934

An item in the N.Y. Times of Sunday reported that a 16 year old Bronx boy was held on a disorderly conduct charge for painting "Vote Communist" on the sidewalk in front of P.S. 50, at Lyons Avenue in the Bronx. The painting was in large red letters. Since neither his political friends or his relatives posted the $25. bond, he spent the night in jail.

66

67

71

73

CHAPTER 8
UPTURN

STOCKS RISE IN RESPONSE TO U.S. DOLLAR POLICY

STOCK MARKET IS UP AFTER CONGRESS VOTES TO REVALUE DOLLAR

JAN. 16, 1934

The financial community responded with enthusiasm on the news that Congress speeded action to support President Roosevelt's request that he be given legislation to devalue the U.S. dollar on the basis of gold reserves.

On Wall Street stocks opened strong and closed up from 1 to 7 points. Trading was more active than it had been since July 21 of last year.

BREADLINES FADE FROM BOWERY

SIGN OF UPTURN IN THE ECONOMY

JAN. 14, 1934

Welfare workers familiar with the Bowery area, which had been the scene of long breadlines on which homeless and out of work men cued up for handouts, report an absence of such lines in recent weeks.

This, in their opinion, is a sign that economic conditions are on the rise. They find that men now have money and are able to care for themselves. Other evidence of the improvement is the growing number of stores in the area with many old buildings being rehabilitated.

JOB RECOVERY REPORT CITES IMPROVEMENT WORLD WIDE

THE UNITED STATES IS LEADING IN GAINS

JAN. 5, 1934

The International Labor office based in Geneva reported that the United States has shown a very marked rise in employment during the last months of 1933. However, unemployment in the U.S. still stood at 10,076,000.

LUMBER PRODUCTION CONTINUES ADVANCE

WEEK ENDING JAN. 13 SHOWS RISE OVER 1933 FOR ORDERS AND ALL LUMBER PRODUCTION

The National Lumber Assn. reported an increase in shipments due to a rise in orders over last year.

80

SHAFTSBURY? SHAFTSBURY?? OUR RUNNER?... WHAT'S HE WANT TO SEE ME ABOUT?

I DON'T KNOW, HE'S WAITING OVER THERE

MR. SMITH, I WANT TO PROPOSE AN IDEA FOR THE FIRM...THERE ARE PROFITS IN BANKRUPTCIES!

SURE ARE LOTS OF THEM THESE DAYS

...I KNOW OF A LUMBER BUSINESS THAT CAN BE **LEVERAGED**...THE UPTOWN BANK IS HOLDING ITS PAPER! I HAVE PEOPLE WHO CAN OPERATE IT...KEEP IT AFLOAT WHILE WE ISSUE STOCK...A PRIVATE PLACEMENT DIVIDED AMONG A FEW INSIDERS...LIKE SPECIAL CLIENTS...AND **US**!!

THEN, AS SOON AS WE HAVE A DECENT BALANCE SHEET—WE **TAKE IT PUBLIC**...AT GOOD MULTIPLES—WE **UNLOAD**! ALL FOR A $5000. INVESTMENT!

WEISS...FIX UP A DESK FOR SHAFTSBURY HERE! HE'S GOING TO WORK ON **NEW ISSUE** UNDERWRITING! ...AND MAKE OUT A CHECK FOR $5000.

81

CHAPTER 9
SANCTUARY

GERMANY RESTRICTS EMIGRATION & TRAVEL

JUNE 28, 1934

In a decree, the German government has restricted travellers to 50 marks in silver — a sum virtually worthless on the foreign exchange. In a second decree it reduced the amount emigrants may take with them to 2000 marks equal to about $650 . . . U.S. currency. In the case of Jews who want to go to Palestine, they may take out a little more — enough to meet the British Mandate regulations. They could also get a little more if they agree to buy German goods when in Palestine.

This, according to a N.Y. Times correspondent, has the effect of stopping all travel outside of Germany for those without funds abroad.

GOEBBELS PUBLISHES CALL TO DISMISS ALL JEWS IN EXPORT FIELD

URGES REPLACEMENT OF 'NON-ARYANS' BY MEN OF "GERMAN RACE"

JAN. 15, 1934

The Nazi anti-semitic program was pushed farther by Dr. Joseph Goebbels, Minister of Propaganda in his newspaper, "Der Angriff." The article said, "It seems intolerable to us that German firms still permit Jews to represent them abroad." He added that those concerned know this and will now make the necessary changes.

REICH TAKES ACTION TO DISCOURAGE ALL MIXED MARRIAGES

MARCH 26, 1934

Berlin: Aryans who married 'non-Aryans' after the Nazi revolution may not use the divorce courts. The journal, German Justice, announced today that unless those who seek to annul such marriages by legal proceedings may do so only if they file during a six month period under the new law. It said, "All those who contracted mixed-marriages after their condemnation by National Socialism placed themselves in opposition to public opinion and will have to bear the consequences of their acts."

NAZIS NOW BAN JEWISH ACTORS

MARCH 7, 1934

Berlin: Anti-Jewish boycotts are now being encouraged officially in Germany. The Nazi organ, "Der Deutsche" has called on all places of entertainment to bar Jewish performers. This follows an order by Dr. Joseph Goebbels to remove all "non-Aryans" from the German stage. S.A. (Storm Troopers) have been stationed at cabaret entrances to enforce the boycott.

U.S. SECRETARY OF LABOR SAYS INCREASED IMMIGRATION NOW WOULD COMPLICATE U.S. UNEMPLOYMENT PROBLEMS

JAN. 30, 1934

Frances Perkins, Secretary of Labor said in a speech today that her Department has been making efforts to "humanize the immigration service." She added that she perceived no sentiment in the country to increase present immigration.

THE N.J. STATE JEWISH WAR VETERANS ASSN. ASKS U.S. TO LOWER IMMIGRATION BARRIERS FOR ALL REFUGEES

MAR. 12, 1934

In a resolution at its annual convention, today, the group called on the United States to permit more German refugees to enter the country.

Mrs. Hilda Fremd.
8 Gaststrasse
Nuremberg, Germany
Dear Hilda;
  I am Jacob Shtarkah the person you wrote about to Rebbe Bensohn. He told me about your trouble and your mother's problem.
  Yes, I remember her very well. Please ask her to write to me right away.
  In the meantime I will ask a friend about bringing her over. Be well.
                    Jacob Shtarkah

Mr. Jacob Shtarkah
55 Dropsie Avenue
Bronx, New York. U.S.A.
Dear Jacob;
  Thank God! My daughter with whom I'm living now gave me your letter. I don't have to tell you how bad things are here. It must be in all the papers. Each day brings worse news. Right now they are leaving my daughter and her husband alone for a little while because he is a doctor and they are not sure if he's Jewish or not. You see his parents are Austrian. So, while they investigate he is still safe.
  I hope to hear from you anything about immigration. I have filed my name at the U.S. Consulate already.
     God bless you
                    Frieda Gold

Mrs. Frieda Gold
In Care of Fremd
8 Gaststrasse
Nuremberg, Germany
Dear Frieda;

I have good News. Elton Shaftsbury, a friend, helped me with a Connection and I filed the papers. Now we must wait! Meanwhile, I am not a rich man but I will be able to afford it for you a passage in case you need. Jacob

Don't forget to get your passport so there won't be a delay

Mr. Jacob Shtarkah
55 Dropsie Avenue
Bronx, N.Y. U.S.A.
Dear Jacob;

God will surely bless you for your kindness. There are new laws here that permit the state to Confiscate Jewish property. Our store was just taken from us. Also, I have to pay a fine because my late husband did not put up a sign on the store saying it was Jewish owned. So I am without any money. I will here to accept your offer to pay my passage. Believe me I will repay you when I get to America. I am not too old to work. Do you remember that weekend we went on a picnic and stopped in that farm house the lady said the same thing when we offered to pay her for food? God bless you, Frieda

86

8... ...asse
Nu...erg, Germany

Dear Frieda;

　　Things are working out fine here so I bought you a ticket — look in this envelope I put it in. Its good for a year so as soon as you get your visa you can leave.

　　Yes, I remember our days in Nuremberg before we parted. Those were happy days. I still remember how you looked. Its 30 years now. Well, I'm sure that you haven't changed as much as I have.

　　So, let me know at once when you are leaving so I can find a place for you to live

　　　　　　Be well,
　　　　　　Jacob

5...
Bronx, NY, USA

Dear Jacob

　　TERRIBLE NEWS!! The police came to look for my daughter and son-in-law. They have proof that he is half-Jewish on his mother's side. Josef (that's his name) and Hilda were in Munich at a medical conference so they're still free — luckily.

　　Please Jacob you must add their names — get them out too — they're in danger. How can I leave without my children?

　　Please try Jacob its getting worse here — you wouldn't believe whats happening!

　　　　　　Frieda

88.

91

CHAPTER 10
AMERICA, AMERICA

JEWISH REFUGEES GET LOCAL HELP

JUNE 15, 1934

The New York Times reported that 259 refugees of the 430 Jews who arrived in New York during May had fled from Nazi Germany. Of these a few came from other countries in Europe where they had fled earlier.

AMERICAN GROUP ASKS U.S. HAVEN FOR NAZI VICTIMS

PRESIDENT ROOSEVELT ASKED TO EASE CURB ON IMMIGRATION

MARCH 19, 1934

Mrs. Carrie Chapman Catt, chairman of a committee of outstanding American women appealed to President Roosevelt for relief from an executive order issued by former President Herbert Hoover restricting immigration. Due to the rigid enforcement of the rules under Hoover beginning in 1930, definite proof that an alien applying for an immigration visa would not become a public charge was very strictly applied. The appeal pointed out that while legal German immigration quotas were 25,959, fewer than 600 had been admitted here in the period from July 1933 to date.

FEWER IMMIGRANTS AT ELLIS ISLAND NOW

JULY 8, 1934

Immigrants arriving in Ellis Island have dwindled in number from 5000 a day to only about 25 in the past 25 years. According to officials this reduced use of the depot is a result of the restrictions on immigration and that most of the aliens coming to settle here pass their technical requirements at the port of embarkation. This permits them to land at piers in this port with other passengers.

AT LONG LAST,

FRIEDA GOLD ARRIVED IN AMERICA.
BEHIND HER WERE THE ASHES OF
A ONCE-SECURE MIDDLE CLASS LIFE
WHERE SHE HAD TAKEN FOR GRANTED...
THE COMFORT OF BELONGING.

95

98

99

101

103

107

108

110

112

116

117

CHAPTER 11
SURVIVAL

MANY MILLIONS OF YEARS AGO... BEFORE THE FAMILIAR FORM OF WHAT WE KNOW AS HUMAN BEINGS APPEARED... THE **COCKROACH**, IN GREAT NUMBERS, INHABITED THE NOOKS AND CRANNIES OF THE EARTH...

IN THE ENSUING CENTURIES THESE INSECTS MANAGED TO SURVIVE LONG AFTER OTHER SIMILAR SPECIES DISAPPEARED!

MEANWHILE, IN A SHORT SPAN OF TIME... THE **HUMAN** SPECIES EVOLVED, AFFECTING THEIR ENVIRONMENT IN A MOST REMARKABLE WAY!!

WONDROUSLY, THESE UPRIGHT CREATURES ACTUALLY CAME TO DEAL WITH AND CONTROL NATURAL PHENOMENA ...THEY WERE ABLE TO DOMINATE OR SUBDUE OTHER FORMS OF LIFE MORE POWERFUL THAN THEY...AND DESPITE FAMINE, DISEASE AND OTHER DISASTERS SUCH AS SELF-DESTRUCTION... THEY HAVE MANAGED TO SURVIVE AND EVEN INCREASE THEIR NUMBERS MANY TIMES OVER!

THEY HAVE, IN COMMON WITH THE COCKROACH, A REMARKABLE LIFE FORCE!

119

122

124

SO, NOW FRIEDA, WE'RE **TOGETHER** AT LAST.

OH, JACOB, THIS IS ONLY ONE ROOM...THE COUCH IS TOO SMALL FOR YOU TO SLEEP HERE

YOU GOT A LITTLE SOUP, MAYBE?

...YOU DON'T UNDERSTAND, FRIEDA...I AM GOING TO DIVORCE RIFKA...WE ARE GOING TO GET MARRIED!

MEANWHILE??

MEANWHILE WE CAN **LIVE TOGETHER**...LATER, I'LL GET A BIGGER APARTMENT I GOT ENOUGH MONEY, THANK GOD, TO TAKE CARE OF YOU...YOU'LL SEE

BUT... RIFKA??

RIFKA??? I'LL SEE TO IT THAT SHE WILL HAVE WHAT TO LIVE ON... FRIEDA...YOUR HAND IS SHAKING...WHY??

127

I'M FRIGHTENED. I DON'T KNOW WHY! *SIGH*: EVERY TIME YOU EXPLAIN, IT SEEMS ALRIGHT...YET, IT'S NOT!

MAKE SENSE, FRIEDA!

IT'S ALL HAPPENING IN SUCH A SHORT TIME...MY WORLD IN GERMANY IS DESTROYED...MY HUSBAND KILLED - MY DAUGHTER RUNNING FROM THE NAZIS - WHO KNOWS WHERE SHE IS? YOU BRING ME TO AMERICA...NOW YOU WANT TO MARRY ME.....

AND NOW WHAT NEXT ??

SO, WHAT ELSE IS THERE ?!

WE'LL ENJOY EACH OTHER... LIVING FROM DAY-TO-DAY

BUT IS THAT ENOUGH ?

BEING GIVEN A SECOND CHANCE IS NO SMALL THING!

...I DON'T KNOW....IS THERE A PURPOSE...A REASON? WHAT DOES GOD WANT FROM ME?

WHO KNOWS ?!

SINCE THE BEGINNING, PRIESTS, RABBIS, GURUS OR GONNIFS...EVERYONE MAKES A BUSINESS OUT OF TRYING TO FIGURE IT OUT! ...THEY WRITE BOOKS AND BIBLES...MAKE UP PRAYERS HOPING, MAYBE, TO GET ONE SMALL ANSWER FROM WHICH THEY CAN GET A CLEAR UNDERSTANDING...AND IN THE MEANTIME - MAN AND COCKROACH JUST LIVE FROM DAY-TO-DAY! WHEN I FIND THE ANSWER, I'LL LET YOU KNOW.

THEN WHAT SHALL WE DO ?

MEANWHILE, WE EAT, SLEEP, AVOID PAIN, ENJOY MAYBE, A LITTLE BEAUTY...AND MAKE LOVE !

128

MAKE LOVE ? ??

JACOB, JACOB,,, I'M 55 YEARS OLD... YOU'RE SIXTY... WE'RE NOT,, I MEAN I CAN'T CATCH FIRE LIKE WHEN I WAS A YOUNG GIRL!

TRY, TRY TO REMEMBER THE FIRST TIME WE... ... IN THE WOODS BACK THEN IN NUREMBERG

YES, AT THE PICNIC.. OH, I WAS SO EXCITED! IT WAS SO BEAUTIFUL THEN!

NOO? ...AND NOW?

AND NOW, I THINK TOO MUCH. NOW I HAVE MORE MEMORIES THAN DREAMS... NOW I CAN ONLY THINK HOW IT WAS WITH MY HUSBAND...

THEN IT WAS A BEAUTIFUL MYSTERY... NO PAST, ONLY THE FUTURE

NOW, IT'S NOT THE SAME... I FEEL LIKE SOME ANIMAL ...WHAT WE ARE TRYING TO DO HERE ISN'T CONNECTED TO HOW I FEEL FOR YOU ...AND YET I DO FEEL SOMETHING FOR YOU JACOB ...

HECH!! SO, THAT'S THE END OF MY FEELING.. ...FEH!

...SHHH.. ITS ENOUGH FOR ME IF YOU JUST HOLD ME, JACOB.

KNOK KNOK

?!

MISSIS GOLD? ARE YOU THE BOOKKEEPER AT LOMBARDI LUMBER YARD... THERE'S BEEN A FIRE THERE... WE FOUND A COUPLA BODIES THERE... WE NEED SOME INFORMATION! JUST ROUTINE ...

129

FIRST OF ALL... THE POLICE REPORT THAT THE FIRE WAS **ACCIDENTAL!** THERE WAS A BRAWL IN WHICH MAX WAS SHOT BY A KNOWN HOODLUM NAMED GINO... HE, TOO, DIED IN THE FIRE!

THIS RULES OUT ARSON... SO, THE INSURANCE COMPANY WILL PAY WITHOUT PROTEST! THIS WILL GIVE YOU SOME MONEY TO REBUILD THE LUMBER YARD!

NOW YOU CAN **MODERNIZE THE PLACE.** PUT IN A SAW FOR CUSTOM MILLING TO MAKE THE YARD MORE PROFITABLE!

...WHICH, BY THE WAY, WILL REASSURE THE STOCKHOLDERS! NOW, WHILE YOUR STOCK WILL DROP SOME ON THE MARKET... THERE WILL **NOT BE A PANIC** SELL-OFF

YOU CAN ALSO PLEDGE SOME OF YOUR STOCK FOR A BANK LOAN... FOR RECONSTRUCTION AND ADVERTISING.. SO, LOMBARDI LUMBER WILL WIND UP AS A **GOOD INVESTMENT**

ELTON, HOW ABOUT PETE AN THE 'HOT' LUMBER ...ARE WE GOIN' TO TAKE THE RAP AS A FENCE?

NO (CHUCKLE) SINCE THE OFFICE BURNED DOWN, ALL THE RECORDS WERE DESTROYED ...SO YOU'RE IN THE CLEAR!!

A CLEAN SLATE, ANGELO!!

Y'HEAR? ...IT'S A NEW START, JACOB ...A NEW START!

131

Dear Rabbi Bensohn;

We have reason to believe that the mother of Hilda Fremd may be known to you. Her name is Frieda Gold. If you can contact her please advise her that her daughter escaped from Germany and is now living in Jerusalem.

She is quite ill, having suffered much during her escape. Her husband was imprisoned by the Nazis and she is without support.

If her mother could be of any financial assistance we would see to it that any funds she can send would be applied for her daughter's benefit.

Yours Truly
JEWISH AGENCY

134

135

137

138

AS FAR AS WE KNOW, THE COCKROACH IS NOT AN ENDANGERED SPECIES. ITS POPULATION ON THE EARTH IS UNRECORDED. ITS PROLIFERATION ON A GLOBAL SCALE SEEMS UNAFFECTED BY THE GROWTH IN HUMAN POPULATION... WHO REGARD IT AS A THREAT TO THEIR NEED FOR A SANITARY ENVIRONMENT.

IN NORTH TEMPERATE ZONES, THE INSECT MOULTS ABOUT 13 TIMES. IT REACHES MATURITY ABOUT SIX MONTHS AFTER HATCHING. IN WARMER CLIMATES IT COMPLETES ITS LIFE CYCLE OVER A PERIOD OF ROUGHLY TWELVE TO THIRTEEN MONTHS. IT SEEMS MAINLY PREOCCUPIED WITH FEEDING AND REPRODUCTION. FOR ALL THEIR LONG INHABITATION OF THIS PLANET THERE IS LITTLE EVIDENCE THAT THE COCKROACH HAS EVOLVED GENETICALLY OR ALTERED ITS LIFE EXPECTANCY. IT HAS AN UNQUESTIONABLE LIFE FORCE EVIDENCED BY ITS WILL TO LIVE!

Will Eisner's career spans the entire history
of comic books from the formative days
of the 1930s, through the 1940s when
he revolutionized narrative sequential art
with his internationally famed series,
THE SPIRIT, to his mature work which,
beginning in the 1970s, led the field
in the creation of the contemporary
graphic novel form.
In addition to his award-winning
graphic novels, he is the author of the
influential study *Comics and Sequential Art.*

If you'd like to learn more about Will Eisner,
visit his website at www.willeisner.com.

the WILL EISNER LIBRARY
FROM DC COMICS

the SPIRIT ARCHIVES
FROM DC COMICS

Will Eisner's The Spirit
collected in chronological order
in full-color, hardcover editions

ALSO BY WILL EISNER